Mr. Mergler, Beethoven, and Me

Inspired by a true story

by David Gutnick

illustrated by Mathilde Cinq-Mars

Second Story Press

Not long after my family arrived from China, I went to the park with my father, whom I call Baba. Lots of people went there to play, enjoy the flowers, and have picnics. That's where I rode my bike, and one special summer morning, it is where I met someone I will always remember.

That Saturday, Baba got so far behind me that I stopped pedaling to let him catch up. I laid my bike down next to a bench where an old gentleman was reading. I went over to the swings and started pumping higher and higher.

From the swing I watched Baba arrive. He sat next to the old man, and pretty soon they were talking. Just as I got as high as the treetops, Baba called me to come over to him.

I dug my heels into the dirt to stop the swing and ran to the bench.

"Say hello to my new friend," Baba said. "This is Mr. Daniel Mergler."

"I am pleased to meet you," I said. My father beamed. He was very proud of my English.

Mr. Mergler shook my hand. Then he pointed past a row of trees. "I live nearby, on the other side of the park. I have been teaching piano lessons there for more than fifty years."

His voice was so soft, I had to lean forward to hear him.

"You see, my mother was a pianist. I used to watch her play, and she looked so happy that it made me happy, too. She taught me piano, and now I teach others."

"Did you teach your own children to play?"
I asked.

Mr. Mergler laughed. "I have taught hundreds of students! Little ones, big ones. They are my children—my own musical family. I have all their pictures on a wall near my piano."

"My daughter plays the piano at our church," Baba told him. "She taught herself."

"Wonderful!" Mr. Mergler smiled at me. "Perhaps you should take lessons."

I looked down at my shoes. Baba worked hard, and we had everything we needed, but I knew there was no extra money for piano lessons.

For a minute no one said anything, and then Mr. Mergler changed the subject.

"Do you have a favorite song you could sing for me?"

"Yes!" I said, and before I knew it, I was singing. "Oh! Susanna, oh don't you cry for me, For I come from Alabama with a banjo on my knee."

While I sang,
Mr. Mergler closed
his eyes and smiled.
He looked so happy
that it made me
happy, too.

When I was finished, Mr. Mergler took a pen and a piece of paper from his pocket. "This is my address," he said to my father. "I would like to teach her to play the piano. Something tells me she understands the magic that music can bring to her life. If she does, that is all the payment I will need."

I couldn't believe my ears. Baba smiled, and his eyes shone as he bowed to Mr. Mergler.

And that is how I became a member of Mr. Mergler's musical family.

The next Sunday, my mother and I walked across the park to Mr. Mergler's studio. The room was dim and cluttered with stacks of books and sheet music. It was as if all the notes in the world were waiting for someone to bring them to life. Near a wall covered with photos stood a large piano. Its ivory keys glowed in the soft light.

"Who is that?" I asked, pointing to the sculpted head of an angry-looking man with wild hair.

"That is Ludwig van Beethoven, a wonderful composer. My aunt gave the bust to me for my ninth birthday, and it has sat on my piano ever since." Mr. Mergler chuckled. "Beethoven went deaf, but I'm sure he still knows when the piano is played well."

At first, the lessons were difficult. I could not figure out how the notes on the page were telling me where to put my fingers.

But Mr. Mergler was patient. He taught me the names of the notes and where they were on the piano.

Before long, understanding where to place my fingers was easy.

Every week, Mr. Mergler gave me a new piece to learn. His pile of music grew smaller as mine grew larger.

When I played with no mistakes, Mr. Mergler gave me a gold star.

"One day," he said, "you will shine more brightly than all these little stars."

I snuck a look at Ludwig van Beethoven. Was it my imagination, or did he look a little more friendly?

My fingers began to fly, and so did my lessons.

Mr. Mergler once told me, "When you are here, seconds, minutes, and hours are part of the outside world. In this room, we get lost in our music, until time itself stands still."

It's like magic, I thought. *We make everything else disappear.* Mr. Mergler and I had twenty-six magical lessons together.

Then one morning at breakfast, my parents were very quiet. I tried not to worry. Instead, I listened to the new piece of music that was playing in my head. But when I noticed tears in Mama's eyes, I knew something was terribly wrong.

"Darling," she said, "Mr. Mergler is very sick."
The music disappeared. Seconds marched past
on the kitchen clock.

Mama and Baba hugged me and took me into the living room. Ludwig von Beethoven was sitting on our piano, and beside him was an envelope with my name on the front. When I opened it, a few gold stars fell to the floor. I read the note.

To my star pupil,

It is so hard to say good-bye. But I am weak and I can't teach anymore.

Here is the phone number of a new teacher. I couldn't leave you without one. He is looking forward to meeting you.

I have given small gifts to many of my children, but you were my best student. Beethoven must come to you. Please keep him on the piano, like I did all my life. He is not so cranky when he is close to good music.

I love you very much.

Remember me always,

Your teacher,

Mr. Mergler

There have been a few changes
since Mr. Mergler died last year.
I have grown taller. I have a new
teacher, and I've learned to play
more difficult compositions.
But some things haven't changed.
Time still disappears when I
practice, and Beethoven still sits
on my piano.

"You heard the music that time, didn't you?"
I whisper, when I have played a piece perfectly.
"I hope Mr. Mergler heard it, too."

Daniel Mergler

Daniel Mergler grew up in a home where music was part of everyday life. His mother would turn on the radio in the living room, and together they would sit on the couch listening to concerts from all over the world. When he was in elementary school, Daniel began piano lessons. He would come home from school and practice because making music made him happy. When he was nine, one of Daniel's aunts gave him a statue of his favorite composer, Ludwig van Beethoven, to put on the top of his piano. After he graduated from university in Montreal, he studied music at the Juilliard School in New York City. Daniel thought about becoming a concert pianist, but he loved the idea of teaching piano even more. And that is what he did for more than fifty years. Daniel's students became members of his family, and even decades after they stopped taking lessons, they stayed in touch. He also wrote poems about music. Daniel Mergler died on May 25, 2003 in Montreal. He was 77 years old.

Ludwig van Beethoven

Ludwig van Beethoven was born in 1770 in Bonn, Germany. Ludwig's father was a singer and he made sure that his son learned to play the organ and the violin. It was soon clear that Ludwig was very talented. He began giving concerts when he was just seven years old. Ludwig found school difficult, and so, when he was ten, he began studying music full-time. By his 20s, Ludwig was famous as an outstanding organist and pianist. He also spent long hours every day composing music. He was not a very friendly man, but people loved listening to his music. Even though he started going deaf when he was in his 30s, he kept writing music. Ludwig van Beethoven died in 1827. He was 56 years old.

Pour Iléana, ma fille superbe,
and Loreen, much adored.
—D.G.

To all the magicians of music
—M.C-M.

Library and Archives Canada Cataloguing in Publication

Gutnick, David, 1956-, author
Mr. Mergler, Beethoven, and me / by David Gutnick ;
illustrated by Mathilde Cinq-Mars.

ISBN 978-1-77260-059-9 (hardcover)

I. Cinq-Mars, Mathilde, 1988-, illustrator II. Title.
III. Title: Mister Mergler, Beethoven, and me.

PS8613.U89M7 2018   jC813'.6   C2017-906252-2

Text ©2018 David Gutnick
Illustrations ©2018 Mathilde Cinq-Mars
Edited by Kathryn Cole
Cover and jacket designed by Ellie Sipila
Interior designed by Melissa Kaita
Printed and bound in China

Second Story Press gratefully acknowledges the support of the
Ontario Arts Council and the Canada Council for the Arts for our
publishing program. We acknowledge the financial support of the
Government of Canada through the Canada Book Fund.

ONTARIO ARTS COUNCIL
CONSEIL DES ARTS DE L'ONTARIO
an Ontario government agency
un organisme du gouvernement de l'Ontario

Canada Council   Conseil des Arts
for the Arts   du Canada

Funded by the Government of Canada
Financé par le gouvernement du Canada

Canadä

Published by
SECOND STORY PRESS
20 Maud Street, Suite 401
Toronto, ON M5V 2M5
www.secondstorypress.ca